HE WHO FINDS A VIRTUOUS WOMAN

By Ukirah Yasmine

To all who realize most never answer this question
in sermons and conversations
because they are focused more on the
qualities of a virtuous woman
than they are on the qualities of a
righteous man who is able to recognize her.

HE WHO FINDS A VIRTUOUS WOMAN

Written By

Ukirah Yasmine

Fullcover Design By

Sun Child Wind Spirit

Proofread By

Summa K. Raynes

Proofread By

Mylia Tiye Mal Jaza

He Who Finds A Virtuous Woman

Softcover ISBN-10: 2853079023

Softcover ISBN-13: 9783138076147

Author Contact
Ukirah Yasmine
Chicago, Illinois
c/o The Writers Consortium
writersconsortium@bepublished.biz

Self-Publishing Associate
BePublished.Org - Chicago
(972) 880-8316
P.O. Box 8324
Jackson, MS 39284
www.bepublished.org
publisher@bepublished.org

First Edition.
Printed In the USA.
Recycled Paper Encouraged.

TABLE OF CONTENTS

(MORE)

TOC (cont'd)

(###)

Poem 1

He Who Finds A Virtuous Woman

Who can find her — so priceless, so rare,
"Her price is far above rubies" declared *(Proverbs 31:10)* — beyond compare.
But the question bends back, not on her alone,
It searches the man whose spirit has grown.

He is not of noise, nor led by demand,
But a man whose life is steady and planned.
For "the heart of her husband safely trusts in her"
(Proverbs 31:11) — it is clear,
Only a secure man can live without fear.

No lack shall he carry, no hunger for gain,
"So that he shall have no need of spoil" *(Proverbs 31:11)* — no striving in vain.
He is full in his being, not empty within,
Not grasping for worth through possession or sin.

He is blessed in her rising, not threatened by light,
"She will do him good and not evil all the days of her life" *(Proverbs 31:12)* — his delight.

For he recognizes favor not as control,
But as the quiet reward of a well-ordered soul.

He walks where honor and wisdom convene,
"Her husband is known in the gates" *(Proverbs 31:23)*
— respected, seen.
Among elders he sits, not by title, but truth,
A man shaped by time, not the haste of youth.

He does not diminish what God has refined,
He does not compete with a virtuous mind.
But lifts what is worthy, speaks what is right,
For her strength adds to his — it does not incite.

"Her children arise up, and call her blessed;
her husband also, and he praises her" *(Proverbs*
31:28) — confessed.
His voice does not tremble, his honor not hide,
He speaks of her worth with unwavering pride.

He is not silent where truth should be known,
He does not reduce what God has grown.
"Many daughters have done virtuously, but thou
excellest them all" *(Proverbs 31:29)* — he will say,
For he knows rare value and will not betray.

He is a giver of credit, not taker of claim,
He does not rewrite what was never his name.
"Give her of the fruit of her hands" *(Proverbs 31:31)* —

he commands,
And lets her works rise and speak in the lands.

In the gates they will echo what he has affirmed,
For honor once spoken is honor confirmed.
He is just in his seeing, aligned in his call,
A man who can recognize — and therefore not fall.

He is not deceived by what fades with the eye,
"Favour is deceitful, and beauty is vain" *(Proverbs 31:30)* — they pass by.
But he discerns deeper, where truth is unfurled,
"A woman that feareth the Lord, she shall be praised" *(Proverbs 31:30)* — his world.

And so he finds her — not by chance, not by scheme,
But by becoming the man fit for the dream.
Not perfect in form, but refined in his way,
A man who has learned what the scriptures convey.

So who can find her? The answer is shown:
The man whose own virtue has steadily grown.
The man who can see, who can trust, who can stand —
Is the one who can find her... and honor her hand.

INTRODUCTION
The Misunderstood Question

There are questions in Scripture that were never meant to be answered quickly.

They were not written for surface readers.
They were not written for casual interpretation.
They were written to separate those who glance from those who discern.

One of those questions is this one found in the Book of Proverbs: *"Who can find a virtuous woman? for her price is far above rubies."* — Proverbs 31:10

For generations, this verse has been quoted, taught, preached, and admired. It has inspired countless sermons, women's studies, conferences, and conversations. Entire identities have been shaped around becoming *the virtuous woman* — as if she were the central mystery of the passage.

But there is something deeply overlooked. Something quietly embedded within the question itself. Something that most readers — though well-intentioned — have missed.

The question was never only about **her**. It was also, and perhaps more profoundly, about **him**.

Question Misplaced

When most people read Proverbs 31, they approach it as a checklist. A standard. A measuring rod for women.

She is to be industrious. She is to be wise. She is to be disciplined, nurturing, resourceful, and strong. And indeed, she is all of these things.

But the question that introduces her is rarely examined with the same intensity: **"Who can find her?"**

Not *where is she*. Not *does she exist*. Not even *how to become her*. But **who can find her**.

This is not a question of location. It is a question of **capacity**.

The Illusion of Scarcity

Over time, this verse has been interpreted to suggest that virtuous women are rare — almost mythical in nature. A precious few among many. A hidden treasure scarcely seen.

But this interpretation, though widely accepted, is incomplete. The rarity is not rooted in her existence. The rarity is rooted in **recognition**.

Because what is truly rare... is not a woman of value. What is rare is a person who can **accurately perceive value** when it does not announce itself loudly.

The virtuous woman described in Proverbs 31 is not loud in her introduction. She is not performative in her excellence. Much of what she does happens in quiet consistency — behind doors, beneath notice, within rhythms that only the discerning eye will appreciate.

Many may see her. But not all will **know what they are seeing**.

Looking Is Not the Same as Finding

There is a difference between looking at something and finding it.

Many look. Few find.

To find something implies more than sight — it implies **recognition, understanding, and readiness**.

A man may encounter a virtuous woman and overlook her completely — not because she is hidden, but because he lacks the depth to interpret what he sees.

In the same way that a person unfamiliar with fine art may walk past a masterpiece without pause, so too can a person lacking spiritual and emotional maturity walk past extraordinary character without comprehension.

The issue is not visibility. The issue is **perception**.

The Silent Presence of the Man

What is most fascinating about Proverbs 31 is that while the passage speaks extensively about the woman, it simultaneously reveals the man — quietly, indirectly, but unmistakably.

He is not described in a single, consolidated statement. He is revealed through:

- What he recognizes
- What he trusts
- What he honors
- Where he is positioned
- And how he speaks of her

He appears in fragments, in glimpses, in actions. But when those fragments are gathered together, a clear picture emerges:

The man who finds a virtuous woman is not ordinary.

He is not shallow. He is not insecure. He is not blind to depth.

He is a man who has been shaped — refined in character, anchored in wisdom, and aligned in spirit.

Because only such a man could not only **see her**... but also **know her worth**.

A Mirror, Not a Pedestal

This book is not written to diminish the value of the virtuous woman. It is written to **restore balance to the conversation**.

For too long, the focus has been placed almost entirely on women becoming worthy — while very little has been said about men becoming capable.

But Scripture does not present value in isolation. It presents **alignment**. A woman who fears the Lord. A man who discerns through wisdom. A partnership built not on appearance, but on **recognition and reverence**.

This book, therefore, is not merely about her. It is a mirror for him. And, in truth, for anyone who seeks to understand what it means to truly *find* something of great worth.

For Those Who Have Felt Unseen

There is also another layer to this message. One that speaks gently, but directly, to those who have ever felt overlooked.

To the women who have wondered: *"If I am who I believe I am... why am I not seen?"*

This book offers a reframing: Perhaps you were not unseen. Perhaps you were **unrecognized**.

And there is a difference. Because being unseen suggests absence.

But being unrecognized suggests that what is present requires a higher level of perception than what was available.

This is not a message of arrogance. It is a message of **clarity**.

The Question, Answered

So we return to the question: **Who can find a virtuous woman?**

Not every man. Not every eye. Not every heart.

But the one who can find her is the one who has become:

- discerning enough to recognize her
- secure enough to trust her

- honorable enough to elevate her
- and aligned enough to walk beside her

In other words: **The man who can find a virtuous woman is the man who has been refined enough to recognize what others overlook.**

This is the foundation of what follows. Not a redefinition of the woman. But a revelation of **the one who can truly find her**.

CHAPTER 1

The Illusion of Scarcity

A common interpretation of Proverbs 31:10 is that the virtuous woman is rare because she is difficult to find in existence. This interpretation has shaped how many approach the passage, leading to the assumption that such women are few and far between. However, this understanding does not fully account for the nature of the question being asked. The verse does not state that she is absent; it asks who is capable of finding her. This distinction shifts the conversation from existence to recognition.

The perception of scarcity often emerges when value is not easily identified. In many areas of life, people tend to equate rarity with absence rather than with a lack of recognition. Something may be present and accessible, yet still be considered rare if few people have the ability to identify it correctly. The same principle applies here. The virtuous woman is not necessarily hidden, but she may not be recognized by those who are not prepared to perceive her accurately.

The qualities described in Proverbs 31 are not superficial. They are rooted in discipline, consistency, wisdom, and responsibility. These traits are not always immediately visible, nor do they always align with what is commonly emphasized or celebrated. In a culture that often prioritizes outward appearance, quick results, and immediate gratification, qualities that develop over time can be overlooked. This does not diminish their value; it simply means they require a different level of attention to be seen.

Misinterpretation also plays a role in the perception of scarcity. Many who claim to be searching for a virtuous woman are, in reality, searching for characteristics that align with their personal preferences rather than the attributes described in the text. When expectations are shaped by superficial standards, it becomes difficult to recognize deeper qualities. As a result, individuals may overlook what they are seeking because they are looking for it in the wrong form.

This creates a cycle in which value is present but unrecognized. A man may encounter a woman who demonstrates wisdom, discipline, and integrity, yet fail to identify her as virtuous because she does not match his expectations. In doing so, he reinforces the belief that such women are rare, when in fact the issue lies in his perception.

The concept of rarity, therefore, must be understood correctly. The virtuous woman is rare not because she does not exist, but because not everyone has developed the ability to recognize her. This reframing places responsibility on the seeker rather than on the subject. It challenges the assumption that the problem lies in the absence of value and instead suggests that it may lie in the inability to perceive it.

Understanding this distinction is essential because it changes the nature of the search. If the issue were truly scarcity, the solution would be to locate what is missing. However, if the issue is recognition, the solution becomes personal development. It requires the seeker to refine his perception, align his values, and cultivate the discernment necessary to identify what he is looking for.

This shift in understanding also addresses the experience of those who feel overlooked. There are women who possess the qualities described in Proverbs 31 yet have not been recognized as such. This reality can lead to questions about their worth or visibility. However, the lack of recognition does not negate their value. It reflects the limitations of those who have encountered them.

The illusion of scarcity persists when recognition is absent. Once perception is corrected, what once seemed rare may be understood as present but previously unrecognized. This is the foundation for understanding the rest of the passage, because it establishes that the question is not about whether she exists, but about who has the capacity to find her.

CHAPTER 2

The Man Who Can See

The ability to see, in the context of this discussion, extends far beyond physical sight. It refers to perception — specifically, the capacity to interpret what is present with clarity, depth, and accuracy. Many people encounter one another daily, yet not all truly see what is before them. This distinction is critical in understanding why the question in Proverbs 31:10 is not about availability, but about recognition.

A man may look at a woman and observe her outward appearance, her demeanor, or her immediate behavior. However, these observations alone do not constitute true perception. To see someone in a meaningful way requires attention to patterns, values, and consistency over time. It requires the ability to move beyond what is immediately visible and engage with what is revealed gradually. Without this level of engagement, a person may form conclusions based on incomplete information, leading to misinterpretation.

Discernment is the mechanism that makes this deeper level of perception possible. It is not an automatic trait, nor is it something that can be assumed simply because one desires it. Discernment is developed through experience, reflection, and a willingness to examine both oneself and others with honesty. It requires patience, because meaningful qualities are not always apparent in initial interactions. It also requires discipline, because it involves resisting the urge to form immediate judgments based on limited evidence.

The virtuous woman described in Proverbs 31 embodies qualities that are revealed through consistency rather than performance. Her discipline is seen in how she manages her responsibilities. Her wisdom is reflected in her speech and decision-making. Her character is demonstrated in how she conducts herself in both visible and private settings. These attributes are not designed to attract attention in a superficial sense; they are the result of a life structured around purpose and principle. As such, they are more easily recognized by someone who values and understands those same principles.

This introduces an important principle: recognition is often limited by familiarity. A person is more likely to identify qualities they have already encountered, studied, or developed within themselves. Conversely, qualities that are unfamiliar or underdeveloped may be misunderstood or overlooked. A man who has not cultivated discipline may not fully appreciate it in another person. A man who has not developed emotional or spiritual depth may struggle to interpret those qualities when he encounters them. This does not reflect a flaw in what he sees, but rather a limitation in how he interprets it.

Observation, therefore, becomes a necessary practice. To see clearly, a man must be willing to observe over time rather than rely on isolated impressions. This involves paying attention to how a person behaves in different contexts, how they respond to challenges, and how they manage responsibilities that are not immediately visible to others. It also involves listening carefully, not only to what is said, but to how it is said and what it reveals about underlying values. Through consistent observation, patterns begin to emerge, and those patterns provide a more accurate understanding than any single moment can offer.

In addition to intellectual and emotional perception, there is also a spiritual dimension to seeing. Scripture consistently emphasizes the importance of wisdom and understanding as foundational to right judgment. The ability to discern character, intention, and alignment is closely tied to one's relationship with God. A man who is grounded in spiritual principles is better equipped to recognize those same principles in others. This alignment does not guarantee perfect judgment, but it does provide a framework through which deeper qualities can be identified.

The absence of this level of perception contributes significantly to the experience described in the previous chapter — the illusion of scarcity. When individuals rely solely on surface-level indicators, they are more likely to overlook qualities that do not present themselves immediately. In doing so, they may conclude that what they are seeking is rare or unavailable, when in reality it has simply not been recognized. This reinforces the idea that the issue is not presence, but perception.

It is also important to acknowledge that seeing carries responsibility. Once a man recognizes value, he is no longer operating from ignorance. He is now aware of what is before him, and that awareness requires a response. Recognition without appropriate action can lead to missed opportunities, while recognition followed by misaligned action can lead to unnecessary strain. Therefore, the ability to see must be accompanied by the willingness to respond with integrity and intention.

The man who can find a virtuous woman is not distinguished by his desire to do so, but by his capacity to perceive what others may overlook. He has developed the patience to observe, the discipline to avoid premature conclusions, and the discernment to interpret what he sees accurately. His perception is not driven by impulse, but by understanding.

In this way, seeing becomes more than an act of observation. It becomes a reflection of development. The ability to recognize value in another person is directly connected to the level of growth within oneself. As a man refines his perception, he increases his ability to identify what is consistent, meaningful, and aligned with the principles described in Proverbs 31.

Understanding this concept provides clarity for both the seeker and the one being sought. It explains why some are overlooked despite possessing strong character, and it highlights the importance of personal development in the process of recognition. Ultimately, the man who can see is not simply one who looks more carefully, but one who has cultivated the depth required to understand what he is looking at.

This foundation leads directly to the next consideration. Recognition establishes awareness, but awareness alone is not sufficient to sustain what has been found. The ability to see must be followed by the ability to trust. Without trust, even the clearest recognition can be undermined by uncertainty and instability.

CHAPTER 3
The Man Who Trusts

Recognition establishes awareness, but awareness alone is not sufficient to sustain what has been found. A man may clearly perceive value, accurately discern character, and correctly identify a virtuous woman, yet still be unable to maintain a relationship with her if he lacks the capacity to trust. For this reason, Proverbs 31 does not only describe what the woman does; it also reveals something essential about the man. It states, “The heart of her husband safely trusts in her” (Proverbs 31:11). This statement is both descriptive and instructive, because it identifies trust as a defining characteristic of the man who is capable of finding her.

The phrase “safely trusts” is particularly important. It does not describe a cautious or conditional trust that is dependent on constant verification. It describes a trust that is stable, secure, and grounded. This type of trust is not easily shaken, nor is it governed by fear. It reflects a man who is internally settled, rather than one who is constantly reacting to uncertainty. Such stability does not emerge automatically; it is developed over time through self-awareness, discipline, and alignment with consistent principles.

A lack of trust often originates from internal instability rather than external evidence. A man who has not resolved his own insecurities may struggle to extend trust even when it is warranted. Past experiences, unresolved fears, or inconsistent personal behavior can all influence how he interprets the actions of others. In such cases, suspicion may arise not because there is a legitimate cause for concern, but because his internal framework is not stable enough to support confidence. This creates a situation in which even a trustworthy person may be treated with doubt.

This distinction highlights an important principle: trust is not solely determined by the behavior of another person; it is also shaped by the condition of the one who is trusting. A man who lacks integrity may find it difficult to believe in the integrity of others. A man who is inconsistent may expect inconsistency from those around him. In this way, perception is influenced not only by observation, but by internal alignment. When alignment is absent, trust becomes difficult to establish, even in the presence of reliability.

The virtuous woman described in Proverbs 31 demonstrates qualities that support trust. She is consistent in her actions, responsible in her duties, and intentional in her decisions. Her behavior reflects discipline and accountability, both of which contribute to a stable environment. However, her reliability alone does not guarantee that she will be trusted. Trust must also be received and sustained by someone who has the capacity to recognize and accept it. Without that capacity, even consistent behavior may be questioned or misunderstood.

This is where the distinction between trust and control becomes significant. Control is often a response to insecurity. It seeks to manage outcomes, reduce uncertainty, and create a sense of stability through external means. Trust, on the other hand, does not rely on constant management. It is based on confidence — confidence in the character of another person and confidence in one's own ability to respond appropriately if circumstances change. A man who cannot trust may attempt to control, not because control is effective, but because it provides a temporary sense of reassurance.

The virtuous woman is not presented as someone who requires control in order to function properly. Her actions already reflect structure, discipline, and responsibility. Attempting to control such a person does not enhance stability; it disrupts it. Control introduces unnecessary tension, while trust allows for continuity and growth. Therefore, the man who is capable of finding her must be able to distinguish between the two and operate accordingly.

Trust also creates an environment in which both individuals can function effectively. When a woman is trusted, she is able to carry out her responsibilities without unnecessary interference. Her decisions are not constantly questioned, and her contributions are not diminished by suspicion. This allows her to operate at the level of consistency and effectiveness described in Proverbs 31. Conversely, when trust is absent, even strong character can be constrained by doubt and misinterpretation.

Sustaining a relationship with a virtuous woman requires more than initial recognition. It requires ongoing stability. A man who is drawn to her strength, discipline, and wisdom must also be able to support those qualities over time. If he is unable to trust, the very attributes that attracted him may eventually become points of tension. Her independence may be misinterpreted as distance, her decisiveness as opposition, and her discipline as rigidity. These misinterpretations are not the result of her behavior changing, but of his inability to maintain a consistent framework of trust.

The phrase “safely trusts” also implies a sense of peace. It suggests that the man is not in a constant state of evaluation or concern. His trust allows him to remain focused, stable, and engaged without being distracted by unnecessary doubt. This does not mean that he is unaware or passive; rather, it means that his awareness is balanced by confidence. He is able to respond when necessary, but he is not governed by the expectation that something will go wrong.

Ultimately, the ability to trust is a reflection of development. It indicates that a man has reached a level of internal stability that allows him to engage with others without projecting unresolved issues onto them. This stability is essential for sustaining any meaningful relationship, but it is particularly important in the context of Proverbs 31, where the woman described operates with a high level of consistency and responsibility.

The man who can find a virtuous woman is not only one who can recognize her; he is one who can trust her without undermining what he has recognized. His trust is not blind, but it is stable. It is informed by observation, supported by alignment, and sustained by his own internal consistency.

This leads to the next essential characteristic. Recognition establishes awareness, and trust provides stability, but neither is complete without expression. The man who is capable of finding her must also be able to honor her — not privately, but in a way that reflects both clarity and confidence in what he has found.

CHAPTER 4

The Man Who Honors

Recognition establishes awareness, and trust provides stability, but neither is complete without expression. A man may clearly perceive value and confidently trust it, yet still fall short of what is required if he does not actively honor what he has found. For this reason, Proverbs 31 does not limit its description to what the woman does or how the man feels about her; it also reveals how he responds. The passage states, "Her children arise up, and call her blessed; her husband also, and he praises her" (Proverbs 31:28), and later, "Give her of the fruit of her hands; and let her own works praise her in the gates" (Proverbs 31:31). These statements make it clear that honor is not internal or implied; it is expressed.

Honor differs from recognition in that it requires visibility. Recognition may exist privately, but honor is demonstrated through words, actions, and consistent acknowledgment. It communicates value in a way that can be observed and understood by others. A man who honors a virtuous woman does not keep his assessment of her to himself. He affirms it openly, ensuring that what he knows to be true is not hidden or minimized.

The emphasis on public acknowledgment is significant. The reference to “the gates” indicates a place of visibility, influence, and communal interaction. In the cultural context of Proverbs, the gates were where leaders gathered, decisions were made, and reputations were established.

For a woman’s works to be praised in that setting, and for her husband to be part of that acknowledgment, suggests that her value is recognized not only in private life but also in broader social contexts. The man associated with her does not obscure her contributions; he affirms them where they can be properly recognized.

This type of response requires a level of internal security. A man who is unsettled within himself may struggle to honor a woman whose strengths are evident. He may perceive her excellence as a point of comparison rather than a shared advantage.

This can lead to subtle forms of resistance, such as minimizing her contributions, withholding acknowledgment, or avoiding situations in which her value would be publicly affirmed. These responses do not arise from a deficiency in the woman, but from a lack of stability in the man.

The man described in Proverbs 31 does not exhibit this instability. His actions indicate that he is not threatened by her capabilities. Instead, he recognizes that her strengths contribute to the overall strength of their partnership. He understands that acknowledging her value does not diminish his own; rather, it reflects positively on both of them. This perspective allows him to speak freely and confidently about her, without hesitation or reservation.

Honor also involves accuracy. To honor someone properly, a man must first understand what he is honoring. This requires attention and discernment. Superficial praise, disconnected from actual behavior, does not constitute true honor.

It may create the appearance of acknowledgment, but it lacks substance. The man who honors a virtuous woman does so based on what he has observed and understood over time. His words align with reality, and his acknowledgment reflects a genuine assessment of her character and contributions.

In addition to verbal affirmation, honor is demonstrated through action. The instruction to "give her of the fruit of her hands" indicates that her work is to be recognized in tangible ways. She is not to be overlooked, nor are her efforts to be absorbed without acknowledgment. Instead, what she has produced is to be attributed to her, and she is to receive the recognition associated with it. This reflects integrity, as it ensures that credit is given where it is due.

The absence of honor can have significant consequences. When value is recognized internally but not expressed externally, it can lead to imbalance. A woman may continue to contribute, build, and support, yet feel that her efforts are not fully acknowledged. Over time, this disconnect between internal recognition and external expression can create strain. It is not that her value has diminished, but that it is not being communicated in a way that reinforces what is already present.

Honor, therefore, plays a critical role in sustaining alignment. It reinforces value, clarifies perception, and strengthens the relationship between recognition and expression. It ensures that what is understood privately is also affirmed publicly, creating consistency between what is known and what is communicated.

The man who honors a virtuous woman does so as a natural extension of what he sees and trusts. His actions are not forced or performative; they are consistent with his understanding. He does not hesitate to speak, nor does he struggle to acknowledge what is evident. His honor is stable, accurate, and visible.

Ultimately, honor completes the progression that has been established thus far. Recognition allows a man to identify value, trust enables him to remain stable in relation to it, and honor ensures that this value is properly expressed and affirmed. Without honor, the process remains incomplete.

The man who can find a virtuous woman is not only capable of seeing and trusting her; he is also willing and able to honor her in a way that reflects both clarity and confidence. His response aligns with what he has recognized, and his acknowledgment reinforces what he has found.

This progression leads to the next characteristic. Recognition, trust, and honor describe how a man perceives and responds, but they do not fully address where he is positioned. Proverbs 31 also provides insight into his environment and standing, indicating that he is known in the gates among others of influence. This positioning is not incidental; it reflects another dimension of the kind of man who is capable of finding her.

CHAPTER 5

The Man Among Gates

Recognition, trust, and honor describe how a man perceives and responds to a virtuous woman, but Proverbs 31 also provides insight into something equally important — his positioning. The passage states, "Her husband is known in the gates, when he sitteth among the elders of the land" (Proverbs 31:23). This detail is not incidental. It reveals that the man who can find a virtuous woman is not only developed internally, but also established externally. His character is reflected not only in private conduct, but in public reputation.

The gates, within the cultural context of the text, represented a place of significance. They were not merely entry points to a city; they functioned as centers of decision-making, discussion, and leadership. Matters of justice, commerce, and governance were addressed there. To be known in the gates was to be recognized among those who carried responsibility and influence. It indicated that a man had a voice that was respected and a presence that was acknowledged by others of similar standing.

This positioning suggests that the man has cultivated a level of consistency and credibility that extends beyond his personal life. He is not defined solely by his private relationships; he is also known for how he conducts himself in broader contexts.

His reputation is not based on isolated moments, but on patterns of behavior that have been observed and evaluated over time. This kind of recognition cannot be manufactured quickly. It is the result of sustained integrity, sound judgment, and responsible action.

Being known in the gates does not necessarily imply wealth or status in a material sense. Rather, it reflects respect. A man may possess resources and still lack credibility, while another may have limited means yet be highly regarded for his wisdom and reliability.

The distinction lies in how he is perceived by those who interact with him in meaningful settings. Respect is earned through consistency, and it is maintained through continued alignment between one's values and actions.

This external positioning is directly connected to the man's ability to recognize value in others. A man who has cultivated wisdom and discernment within himself is more likely to identify those same qualities in someone else. His exposure to thoughtful discussion, responsible decision-making, and principled living provides him with a framework for evaluation. He is not easily misled by appearances, because his environment reinforces the importance of substance over presentation.

In contrast, a man who is not positioned among those who value wisdom may lack the context necessary to recognize it. If his environment prioritizes superficial measures of success or immediate gratification, his perception may be shaped accordingly. This does not mean that he is incapable of growth, but it does suggest that his current framework may not support accurate recognition of deeper qualities. Environment plays a significant role in shaping both perception and expectation.

The connection between positioning and recognition also highlights the importance of alignment. The virtuous woman described in Proverbs 31 operates with discipline, foresight, and intentionality. She manages resources, engages in productive work, and contributes to the well-being of her household and community. A man who is positioned among the wise is more likely to understand and appreciate these qualities, because they align with the principles he encounters in his own sphere of influence.

Furthermore, being known in the gates implies accountability. A man who sits among others of influence is subject to observation and evaluation. His decisions, speech, and conduct are not isolated; they are part of a broader network of interactions.

This accountability reinforces discipline, as it requires him to maintain consistency in various contexts. It also contributes to his credibility, as others come to recognize his reliability over time.

This level of positioning also affects how he responds to the woman he has found. A man who is accustomed to environments that value integrity is less likely to diminish or overlook those qualities in his personal relationships.

He understands the importance of acknowledging what is genuine and sustaining what is valuable. His public and private lives are not disconnected; they reflect a unified approach to character and responsibility.

It is also important to note that being known in the gates does not mean that a man is without growth areas or challenges. Rather, it indicates that he has reached a level of development where his contributions are meaningful and his presence is respected. Growth continues, but it occurs within a framework that already supports stability and discernment.

The inclusion of this detail in Proverbs 31 reinforces the broader principle that the man who can find a virtuous woman is not defined by a single trait. He is not only perceptive, trusting, and honoring; he is also positioned in a way that reflects his development. His environment, reputation, and interactions all contribute to his ability to recognize and sustain what he has found.

Ultimately, positioning among the wise enhances perception. It provides a context in which value is more easily identified and appreciated. It also reinforces the importance of consistency, as a man's reputation is built on observable patterns rather than isolated actions. This alignment between internal development and external positioning is essential for understanding the kind of man described in the passage.

As the text continues to unfold, another foundational characteristic becomes clear. While positioning among the wise reflects external credibility, it is rooted in something deeper. The ability to maintain wisdom, discernment, and consistency is closely tied to one's relationship with God. This leads to the next defining trait: the man who can find a virtuous woman is a man who fears God.

CHAPTER 6

The Man Who Fears God

Recognition, trust, honor, and positioning all describe essential qualities of the man who can find a virtuous woman, but none of these qualities stand independently. They are not isolated traits that develop at random. They are rooted in a deeper foundation — one that governs perception, stabilizes character, and aligns judgment. That foundation is the fear of God.

The Book of Proverbs consistently establishes this principle. Proverbs 9:10 states, "The fear of the Lord is the beginning of wisdom." This is not presented as an optional attribute, but as the starting point from which understanding develops. Without this foundation, other qualities may appear in fragments, but they lack consistency and depth. With it, discernment becomes sharper, judgment becomes more reliable, and character becomes more stable.

To fear God does not mean to exist in a constant state of anxiety or dread. It refers to reverence, alignment, and an awareness of accountability that extends beyond human observation. It is the recognition that one's actions, decisions, and intentions are not solely evaluated by others, but are also measured against a higher standard. This awareness shapes behavior, not through external pressure, but through internal conviction.

A man who fears God approaches life with a sense of order. His decisions are not based solely on impulse or preference, but on principles that remain consistent regardless of circumstance. This consistency influences how he perceives others. He is not easily distracted by superficial qualities, because his framework for evaluation is not built on appearance or immediate gratification. Instead, he is oriented toward substance, alignment, and long-term stability.

This orientation is essential in recognizing a virtuous woman. Proverbs 31:30 states, "Favour is deceitful, and beauty is vain: but a woman that feareth the Lord, she shall be praised." The defining characteristic of the woman is not external appeal, but her reverence for God. This creates a point of alignment between her and the man who is capable of finding her. Without this shared foundation, recognition becomes inconsistent, and the ability to sustain the relationship is weakened.

Alignment in this context is not merely agreement in belief; it is consistency in practice. A man who fears God demonstrates it through his actions, his speech, and his decisions. His reverence is not confined to private moments; it is reflected in how he conducts himself in all areas of life. This consistency allows him to recognize similar patterns in others. When he encounters a woman whose life reflects the same foundation, he is able to identify it not as an abstract concept, but as a lived reality.

The absence of this foundation can lead to misinterpretation. A man who does not operate from a place of reverence may still recognize certain qualities, but he may not understand their significance. He may appreciate discipline without understanding its purpose, or admire consistency without recognizing its source. Without a framework that connects these qualities to a deeper principle, his perception remains incomplete. This increases the likelihood that he will overlook or undervalue what he encounters.

The fear of God also contributes to stability. A man who is aligned with consistent principles is less likely to be influenced by changing circumstances or external pressures. His decisions are guided by a standard that does not fluctuate, which allows him to remain steady in his perception and response. This stability is essential when engaging with a woman whose life is also structured around discipline and purpose. It creates an environment in which both individuals can operate with clarity and consistency.

In addition, reverence for God introduces accountability. A man who recognizes that his actions are subject to a higher standard is more likely to approach relationships with responsibility and intention. He understands that recognition, trust, and honor are not merely personal choices, but reflections of his alignment with that standard. This awareness influences how he treats others, ensuring that his actions are consistent with his stated values.

It is also important to note that the fear of God is not static. It is developed and strengthened over time through reflection, study, and intentional practice. A man who is growing in this area becomes more refined in his perception and more consistent in his behavior. This ongoing development enhances his ability to recognize and sustain what is valuable.

The connection between reverence and recognition reinforces the central theme of this book. The question, "Who can find a virtuous woman?" is not answered by identifying her location, but by examining his condition. A man who fears God is positioned to recognize a woman who fears God, because their frameworks are aligned. This alignment reduces misinterpretation and increases the likelihood of accurate perception.

Ultimately, the fear of God serves as the foundation upon which the other characteristics rest. It informs discernment, supports trust, enables honor, and reinforces credibility. Without it, these qualities may appear in limited forms, but they lack the consistency required to sustain a relationship with a virtuous woman.

This foundation leads to an important realization. If these characteristics are required to recognize and sustain what is described in Proverbs 31, then it follows that not everyone will possess them. This brings the discussion to the next consideration: why many are unable to find her, not because she is absent, but because the necessary development has not yet occurred.

CHAPTER 7

Why Many Cannot Find Her

If the virtuous woman is not absent, and if her qualities are clearly described, then the question must be asked: why do so many claim they cannot find her? The answer does not lie in her scarcity, but in the condition of those who are searching. The inability to find her is not primarily a matter of location or opportunity; it is a matter of development, perception, and alignment.

Throughout the previous chapters, a consistent pattern has been established. The man who can find a virtuous woman is one who can see with discernment, trust with stability, honor with confidence, position himself among the wise, and operate from a foundation of reverence for God. These characteristics are not superficial, nor are they acquired without intention. They require growth, discipline, and self-examination. When these elements are absent, recognition becomes difficult, even when what is being sought is present.

One of the primary barriers to recognition is immaturity. Immaturity is not defined solely by age, but by a lack of development in judgment, responsibility, and self-control. A man who has not cultivated these qualities may approach relationships with expectations that are inconsistent with the characteristics described in Proverbs 31. He may prioritize immediate gratification over long-term stability, or surface-level appeal over substantive character. In doing so, he creates a framework that is incompatible with what he claims to be seeking.

Ego also plays a significant role. An inflated sense of self can distort perception by placing personal preference above objective evaluation. A man governed by ego may struggle to recognize value that does not align with his expectations, or he may resist acknowledging qualities that challenge his sense of control or superiority. This resistance can lead to dismissal or misinterpretation, not because the value is absent, but because it does not conform to his perspective.

Another factor is the lack of discipline. The virtuous woman described in Proverbs 31 operates with consistency and intentionality. Her actions reflect structure and responsibility. A man who lacks discipline may find it difficult to relate to or sustain a connection with someone who embodies these qualities. What should be recognized as stability may instead be perceived as rigidity, and what should be valued as consistency may be interpreted as monotony. These misinterpretations arise not from her behavior, but from his lack of alignment.

Misaligned desires further complicate the issue. Many individuals seek qualities that are immediately appealing but not necessarily enduring. When preferences are shaped by temporary or superficial standards, deeper qualities may be overlooked. This creates a disconnect between what is desired and what is needed. A man may claim to be searching for a virtuous woman while simultaneously prioritizing characteristics that are unrelated to virtue. This inconsistency makes accurate recognition unlikely.

Environmental influence also contributes to the inability to find her. The context in which a person operates shapes both perception and expectation. If a man is consistently exposed to environments that prioritize appearance, status, or short-term satisfaction, his understanding of value may be influenced accordingly. Without exposure to different standards, he may lack the framework necessary to identify qualities that do not align with those influences. This does not make recognition impossible, but it does make it more challenging.

In addition to these factors, there is the issue of readiness. Recognition requires not only the ability to perceive, but also the ability to respond appropriately. A man may encounter a virtuous woman and recognize certain qualities, yet still be unprepared to engage with her in a meaningful way. Readiness involves emotional stability, clarity of intention, and the capacity to sustain what has been identified. Without these elements, recognition may occur without resulting in a lasting connection.

It is also important to consider the role of projection. Individuals often interpret others through the lens of their own experiences, assumptions, and unresolved issues. This can lead to misjudgment, as behaviors are assigned meanings that do not accurately reflect their intent. A man who has experienced inconsistency may expect it, even when it is not present. A man who has encountered dishonesty may approach new situations with suspicion. These projections can obscure accurate perception, making it difficult to recognize what is actually there.

The cumulative effect of these factors is a pattern of missed recognition. Value is encountered but not identified, or identified but not understood. Over time, this pattern can reinforce the belief that what is being sought is rare or nonexistent. However, this conclusion does not account for the underlying causes of the missed recognition. It attributes the outcome to absence rather than to the limitations of perception and readiness.

Understanding why many cannot find her is essential because it shifts responsibility from the subject to the seeker. It challenges the assumption that the problem lies in the availability of virtuous women and instead highlights the importance of personal development. This perspective does not assign blame; it identifies areas for growth. It suggests that the ability to find what one is seeking is directly related to the effort invested in becoming capable of recognizing it.

This realization also provides clarity for those who have felt overlooked. If the inability to find her is rooted in the condition of the seeker, then being unrecognized does not indicate a lack of value. It indicates a mismatch between what is present and what is perceived. This distinction is important because it reframes the experience of being overlooked as a reflection of misalignment rather than deficiency.

Ultimately, the question of why many cannot find her is answered by examining the requirements for recognition and the extent to which those requirements have been met. When discernment, trust, honor, positioning, and reverence are absent or underdeveloped, the likelihood of accurate recognition decreases. When these qualities are cultivated, the ability to find what is valuable increases.

This understanding leads to the next stage of the discussion. If the inability to find her is rooted in a lack of development, then the logical response is not continued searching without change, but intentional growth. The focus must shift from external pursuit to internal refinement. The next chapter addresses this directly by examining what it means to become the kind of person who is capable of finding what has already been described.

CHAPTER 8

The Burden of Being Unrecognized

The discussion thus far has focused primarily on the one who seeks, examining the qualities required to recognize a virtuous woman. However, there is another side to this reality that must be addressed — the experience of those who possess the qualities described in Proverbs 31 yet remain unrecognized. While the inability to find her is often attributed to her supposed rarity, the lived experience of many women suggests a different conclusion. They are present, consistent, and aligned with the principles described, yet they are overlooked, misunderstood, or undervalued.

This experience creates a unique burden. It is not the burden of lacking value, but the burden of existing in environments where value is not properly perceived. Over time, this can lead to confusion, as repeated instances of being overlooked may be interpreted as evidence of deficiency rather than misalignment. Questions begin to arise: Is something missing? Is there something that needs to be changed? These questions are not inherently problematic, but they can become misleading if they are based on inaccurate assumptions about the cause of the experience.

Being unrecognized is not the same as being invisible. Visibility implies that something cannot be seen at all, whereas recognition involves interpretation. A person may be clearly visible yet not understood. In the context of this discussion, the virtuous woman is not hidden. Her actions, decisions, and patterns are observable. However, without the appropriate framework for interpretation, those observations may not lead to accurate conclusions. This distinction is critical because it separates presence from perception.

The burden of being unrecognized is compounded when external feedback reinforces the misinterpretation. In environments where superficial qualities are prioritized, deeper attributes may not receive acknowledgment. This can create a disconnect between internal reality and external response. A woman may be operating with discipline, wisdom, and intentionality, yet receive little recognition for these qualities because they do not align with what is immediately celebrated. Over time, this disconnect can create tension, as the absence of acknowledgment may be mistaken for the absence of value.

It is important to understand that recognition is not solely determined by the presence of qualities, but by the capacity of the observer. As established in previous chapters, the ability to perceive value requires discernment, alignment, and development. When these elements are absent, even clear indicators of character may be overlooked. This does not diminish the reality of the qualities present; it highlights the limitations of the environment in which they are being observed.

The temptation in such situations is to adjust in order to be recognized. This may involve altering behavior, emphasizing more visible traits, or deprioritizing qualities that are not immediately acknowledged. While adaptation can be useful in certain contexts, it becomes problematic when it leads to a departure from foundational principles. The virtuous woman described in Proverbs 31 is consistent, not because she is resistant to growth, but because her actions are rooted in values that do not change based on external validation. To abandon those values for the sake of recognition would undermine the very qualities that define her.

Another aspect of this burden is the misinterpretation of consistency. In a culture that often values novelty and variation, consistent behavior can be perceived as predictable or unremarkable. However, consistency is one of the defining characteristics of reliability. It reflects discipline and intentionality, both of which are essential for sustaining long-term outcomes. The lack of recognition for consistency does not reduce its importance; it indicates that the observer may be prioritizing different criteria.

The experience of being unrecognized can also affect how one interprets future interactions. Repeated instances of being overlooked may lead to increased caution or reduced expectation. While this can serve as a protective measure, it may also limit openness to new opportunities. It is therefore important to maintain clarity regarding the source of the experience. If the issue is misalignment rather than deficiency, then the appropriate response is not withdrawal, but continued alignment with one's values while remaining attentive to environments and individuals capable of accurate recognition.

This perspective also reframes the concept of timing. Recognition is not always immediate, and it is not guaranteed in every context. The alignment required for accurate perception may not be present in every interaction. This does not imply that recognition will not occur; it suggests that it is contingent upon encountering individuals who possess the necessary framework for understanding. Timing, therefore, is not solely a matter of sequence, but of alignment between presence and perception.

It is also necessary to address the role of self-assessment. While being unrecognized may often reflect external limitations, it is still important to engage in honest evaluation. This ensures that the conclusion of misalignment is not used to avoid areas where growth is needed. The distinction lies in the basis of the assessment. When evaluation is grounded in objective criteria and consistent principles, it contributes to development. When it is based solely on external response, it may lead to unnecessary adjustment.

Ultimately, the burden of being unrecognized is a result of operating at a level that is not universally perceived. This does not make the position superior or inferior; it makes it specific. It requires alignment with individuals who have developed the capacity to recognize and engage with those qualities. Until that alignment occurs, the experience of being overlooked may continue, not as a reflection of absence, but as a consequence of mismatch.

Understanding this dynamic provides clarity and direction. It removes the assumption that value must be altered in order to be acknowledged and replaces it with the understanding that recognition depends on the readiness of the observer. This shift allows for continued consistency without unnecessary compromise.

The discussion now returns to the central theme of development. If recognition is dependent on the condition of the seeker, then the focus must be placed on what it means to become capable of finding what has been described. The next chapter addresses this directly by examining the process of becoming the one who can find a virtuous woman.

CHAPTER 9

Becoming the One Who Can Find

If the inability to find a virtuous woman is rooted not in her absence but in the condition of the seeker, then the solution cannot be found in continued searching alone. It must be found in development. The question shifts from "Where is she?" to "Who must I become in order to recognize her?" This shift is essential because it places responsibility on personal growth rather than external circumstances.

Becoming the one who can find a virtuous woman is not a matter of adopting isolated traits or imitating behaviors. It involves a comprehensive process of refinement that affects perception, decision-making, and conduct. This process requires intentional effort, as the qualities necessary for accurate recognition do not develop without direction. They are cultivated through consistent practice, reflection, and alignment with stable principles.

The first aspect of this development is discernment. As established earlier, discernment is the ability to interpret what is present with clarity and depth. Developing discernment requires exposure to sound principles and a willingness to apply them consistently. It also requires patience, as accurate perception is often the result of observation over time rather than immediate judgment. A man who seeks to develop discernment must be willing to evaluate his assumptions, refine his understanding, and resist the impulse to draw conclusions based on limited information.

Alongside discernment is the development of internal stability. Trust, as described in Proverbs 31:11, is not sustainable without a stable foundation. This stability is achieved through self-awareness and discipline. It involves recognizing areas of inconsistency and addressing them directly. A man who is internally stable is less likely to project unresolved issues onto others, and more likely to respond to situations with clarity rather than reaction. This stability allows him to engage with others without undermining what he has recognized.

Honor also requires development. To honor someone properly, a man must be both willing and able to express acknowledgment in a way that is accurate and consistent. This involves overcoming tendencies toward silence, hesitation, or discomfort in recognizing the contributions of others. It also requires integrity, ensuring that acknowledgment is not selective or conditional, but aligned with observed reality. Developing the capacity to honor strengthens relationships by reinforcing value and creating alignment between perception and expression.

Positioning is another critical component. As discussed in the previous chapters, being known among the wise contributes to both perception and credibility. This positioning is not achieved through status alone, but through consistent engagement with environments that prioritize sound judgment and responsible action. A man who seeks to develop in this area must be intentional about the contexts in which he participates. Exposure to environments that value substance over appearance supports the development of discernment and reinforces consistent behavior.

The fear of God remains the foundation upon which these developments rest. Without this foundation, growth may occur in isolated areas, but it lacks cohesion. Reverence for God provides a consistent standard that informs decisions, shapes behavior, and aligns priorities. It ensures that development is not driven solely by personal preference, but by principles that remain stable over time. This alignment is essential for sustaining the qualities necessary to recognize and engage with a virtuous woman.

The process of becoming also involves the evaluation of desires. Misaligned desires can distort perception, leading to the prioritization of qualities that do not support long-term stability. A man must examine what he values and determine whether those values align with the characteristics described in Proverbs 31. This evaluation may require adjustment, as preferences shaped by external influences may not reflect what is necessary for a meaningful and sustained relationship.

Discipline is required to maintain this alignment. Development is not a one-time event, but an ongoing process. It involves consistent application of principles, even when circumstances change. This consistency reinforces stability and strengthens perception, allowing for more accurate recognition over time. Without discipline, progress may be inconsistent, and the ability to sustain what has been developed may be compromised.

It is also important to recognize that becoming does not imply perfection. The man who can find a virtuous woman is not without flaws or areas for growth. However, he has reached a level of development that allows him to perceive, trust, honor, and align with what he encounters. His growth is ongoing, but it is structured and intentional. This structure provides the stability necessary to engage with others in a meaningful way.

The process of becoming has implications beyond recognition. It influences how a man responds once he has identified what he is seeking. Without the necessary development, recognition may not lead to a sustainable outcome. With it, recognition can be followed by appropriate action, creating the conditions for a stable and aligned relationship. This underscores the importance of focusing on development rather than solely on pursuit.

Understanding this process also clarifies the relationship between effort and outcome. Finding a virtuous woman is not achieved through effort directed outward alone. It is the result of effort directed inward, leading to a state in which recognition becomes possible. This does not eliminate the need for interaction or engagement, but it ensures that those interactions are informed by clarity and alignment.

Ultimately, becoming the one who can find a virtuous woman is a process of refinement. It involves aligning perception, stabilizing character, and grounding behavior in consistent principles. This alignment increases the likelihood of accurate recognition and supports the ability to sustain what has been found.

This progression leads to the final stage of the discussion. When recognition, trust, honor, positioning, and reverence are aligned, and when development has occurred, the conditions are established for a meaningful encounter. The next chapter examines what happens when readiness meets recognition, and how alignment influences the outcome of that meeting.

CHAPTER 10

When Recognition Meets Readiness

Throughout this discussion, a consistent principle has been established: the ability to find a virtuous woman is not determined by her absence or presence alone, but by the condition of the one who seeks her. Recognition requires discernment, stability, alignment, and development. However, there is a final element that must be considered — the moment when these qualities converge. What happens when recognition meets readiness?

This moment is often misunderstood because it is frequently framed in terms of chance or timing alone. While timing plays a role, it is not the sole determining factor. Recognition without readiness may lead to awareness without action, while readiness without recognition may result in missed opportunities. The alignment of both elements creates the conditions under which a meaningful and sustained connection can occur.

When a man who has developed the necessary qualities encounters a woman who embodies the characteristics described in Proverbs 31, the interaction is not governed by confusion or uncertainty. His perception is informed by discernment, allowing him to identify her qualities with clarity. His internal stability supports trust, preventing unnecessary doubt or misinterpretation. His capacity for honor ensures that his recognition is expressed appropriately. His positioning among the wise reinforces his understanding, and his reverence for God aligns his actions with consistent principles.

This alignment creates a different kind of interaction. It is not driven by impulse or external pressure, but by understanding. The man does not need to rely on assumptions or incomplete information, because his perception has been developed. He is able to engage with intention, recognizing both the significance of what he has encountered and the responsibility that comes with it.

For the woman, this encounter also reflects alignment. Her consistency, discipline, and reverence are not new developments; they are established aspects of her character. When she encounters someone who is capable of recognizing these qualities, the interaction is marked by clarity rather than confusion.

She is not required to alter her behavior to be understood, nor does she need to reduce her standards to accommodate misalignment. The recognition she receives is consistent with what she has demonstrated.

This convergence reduces the likelihood of misinterpretation. When both individuals operate from aligned principles, their actions and decisions are informed by similar frameworks. This does not eliminate all challenges, but it provides a stable foundation for addressing them.

Differences can be evaluated within a shared context, and decisions can be made with reference to consistent standards. This alignment supports continuity, allowing the relationship to develop without the instability that often arises from mismatched expectations.

It is important to note that readiness does not guarantee immediate recognition in every situation, nor does recognition guarantee immediate alignment. External factors, such as environment and timing, can still influence outcomes. However, when both recognition and readiness are present, the likelihood of a meaningful connection increases significantly.

The interaction is no longer dependent on chance alone; it is supported by preparation and alignment.

This perspective also clarifies the role of timing. Timing is often perceived as a sequence of events, but it is more accurately understood as the intersection of development and opportunity. A man may encounter a virtuous woman before he has developed the capacity to recognize her, or he may develop that capacity after the opportunity has passed. In both cases, timing is not simply a matter of when the encounter occurs, but of whether the necessary conditions are present at that moment.

When recognition meets readiness, the interaction is characterized by intentionality. The man approaches with clarity, the woman responds with consistency, and both operate within a framework that supports understanding. This does not eliminate the need for continued effort, but it ensures that the effort is directed appropriately. The relationship is not built on assumptions or adjustments made to compensate for misalignment, but on a foundation that reflects what has already been established in each individual.

The convergence of these elements also reinforces the central theme of this book. The question, “Who can find a virtuous woman?” is answered not by identifying her location, but by examining the conditions under which recognition becomes possible. When a man has developed the necessary qualities, and when those qualities align with what he encounters, the process of finding becomes clear. It is no longer defined by uncertainty, but by understanding.

This understanding extends beyond the initial encounter. Sustaining what has been found requires the continued application of the same principles that made recognition possible.

Discernment must remain active, trust must remain stable, honor must remain consistent, positioning must be maintained, and reverence must continue to guide decisions. The alignment that initiated the connection must be preserved in order to support its development over time.

Ultimately, when recognition meets readiness, the question is resolved. The virtuous woman is not discovered through chance, but through alignment.

The man who finds her does so because he has become capable of recognizing what others may overlook, and he is prepared to respond in a way that reflects that understanding.

This brings the discussion to its conclusion. The principles outlined throughout this book are not isolated observations, but interconnected elements that together define the answer to the question posed in Proverbs 31:10. The final section will reflect on this answer and reinforce the central idea that has guided this exploration from the beginning.

CONCLUSION

The Answer Was Never Hidden

The question that began this discussion has been asked for generations: "Who can find a virtuous woman?" It has been quoted, interpreted, and repeated across contexts, often with the assumption that it refers to scarcity. The prevailing belief has been that such a woman is difficult to find because she is rare in existence. However, as this examination has shown, the question does not point to her absence. It points to the condition of the one who seeks her.

The description provided in Proverbs 31 is not ambiguous. It outlines a woman who is disciplined, intentional, wise, and consistent. Her actions reflect responsibility, foresight, and alignment with principles that extend beyond immediate circumstances. These qualities are observable, but they are not always immediately recognized. They require discernment, patience, and an understanding that extends beyond surface-level evaluation.

The central issue, therefore, is not whether she exists, but whether she is correctly identified. Recognition depends on perception, and perception is shaped by development. A man who has cultivated discernment is able to interpret what he observes with greater accuracy. A man who has developed internal stability is able to trust without projecting insecurity. A man who operates with integrity is able to honor what he recognizes without hesitation. A man who is positioned among the wise is supported by an environment that reinforces sound judgment. A man who fears God is guided by a consistent standard that informs his decisions and aligns his perception.

These elements are not independent. They form a cohesive framework that determines the ability to recognize and sustain what has been found. When this framework is absent, recognition becomes inconsistent, and value may be overlooked. When it is present, the process of finding becomes clear. The question is answered not through external search, but through internal alignment.

This perspective also reframes the experience of those who have felt unseen. Being overlooked does not necessarily indicate a lack of value. It may reflect a lack of alignment between what is present and what is perceived. This distinction is important because it removes the assumption that value must be altered in order to be recognized. Instead, it highlights the role of perception and the importance of encountering individuals who have developed the capacity to understand what is before them.

The progression outlined throughout this book demonstrates that finding is not a single event, but the result of a process. It begins with perception, continues with trust, is expressed through honor, is reinforced by positioning, and is grounded in reverence. Each of these elements contributes to the ability to recognize and sustain what has been described in Proverbs 31. Without them, the process remains incomplete. With them, the question is resolved.

It is also important to recognize that this process is ongoing. Development does not end once recognition occurs. The same qualities that enable a man to find a virtuous woman are required to maintain alignment over time. Discernment must continue to guide perception, stability must continue to support trust, honor must continue to be expressed, positioning must continue to reflect integrity, and reverence must continue to provide direction. Sustaining what has been found requires the same level of intentionality that made recognition possible.

The question, then, is not one that demands a complex or hidden answer. It is straightforward when understood in its proper context. The man who can find a virtuous woman is the one who has become capable of recognizing her. His development determines his perception, and his perception determines his ability to identify what is present.

This understanding brings clarity to a passage that has often been misunderstood. It shifts the focus from external search to internal preparation, from assumed scarcity to developed recognition. It reveals that the answer has not been concealed, but has remained visible within the text itself.

The question was never meant to lead to speculation about her existence. It was meant to direct attention to the qualities required to perceive her. Once those qualities are understood and developed, the process of finding is no longer defined by uncertainty.

The answer was never hidden. It was always present, waiting to be recognized by those who were prepared to see it.

next

Poem 2

He Who Can Find Her

Who can find her —
the woman whose worth is named in rubies,
whose days rise before the sun
and whose hands do not forget their work?
The question was never empty.
It was never wandering.
It was aimed — precise —
at the man who must become
what his eyes are asking to see.
(Proverbs 31:10)

He is not merely one who looks.
Many have eyes.
Many have desire.
Many speak of what they seek.
But Scripture does not ask who is searching —
it asks who can **find**.

And the answer is written
not in one place,
but scattered like truth
for the one who reads with care.

He is a man of understanding,
not hurried in judgment,
not shallow in sight.
For "counsel in the heart of man is like deep water;
but a man of understanding will draw it out."
(Proverbs 20:5)

He does not skim the surface of a life
and call it knowing.
He draws.
He waits.
He listens beneath words
until meaning rises.

He sees what others pass by.
Not because she is hidden —
but because he is trained.

He is rooted, not restless.
His life is not blown
by every shifting wind of desire.
"But his delight is in the law of the Lord...
and he shall be like a tree planted by the rivers of water,
that bringeth forth his fruit in his season."
(Psalm 1:2–3)

He does not chase
what cannot sustain him.
He recognizes life
because he is planted in it.

And when he finds her,
his response is not suspicion.

It is trust.

Not fragile.
Not conditional.
Not temporary.

“The heart of her husband safely trusts in her.”
(Proverbs 31:11)

Safely —
because he is not governed by fear.
Safely —
because he is not divided within himself.
Safely —
because what is stable in him
recognizes what is stable in her.

He does not attempt to control
what is already disciplined.
He does not question
what has already proven itself.

He does not shrink
in the presence of her strength.

For he is not threatened by what is whole.

He stands where wisdom gathers.

"Her husband is known in the gates,
when he sitteth among the elders of the land."
(Proverbs 31:23)

He is not unknown among men of weight.
Not because of title,
but because of consistency.
Because his words carry thought.
Because his presence carries measure.
Because his life has been observed
and found steady.

He is a man who has learned
that reputation is not declared —
it is built.

And when he speaks of her,
he does not lower his voice.

He does not hide his recognition
as if her value were a secret.

"Her husband also, and he praises her."
(Proverbs 31:28)

He speaks what he sees.
He affirms what is evident.
He does not compete
with what he has been given.

"Give her of the fruit of her hands;
and let her own works praise her in the gates."
(Proverbs 31:31)

He does not take what she has built
and rename it as his own.
He does not silence her evidence
to protect his ego.

He understands
that honor is not loss.

It is alignment.

And beneath all of this —
beneath his sight,
his trust,
his speech,
his position —

there is a foundation.

"The fear of the Lord is the beginning of wisdom."
(Proverbs 9:10)

This is where he begins.
Not with preference.
Not with impulse.
Not with assumption.

But with reverence.

And so when he sees her —
truly sees her —
he recognizes what defines her:

"A woman that feareth the Lord, she shall be praised."
(Proverbs 31:30)

He knows that language.
He knows that life.
He knows that pattern.

Because he lives by it too.

So who can find her?

Not every man who searches.
Not every man who desires.
Not every man who claims to be ready.

But the one who has become
what the question requires.

The one who can see
beyond appearance.
The one who can trust
without fear.
The one who can honor
without hesitation.
The one who is established
among the wise.
The one who is grounded
in the fear of the Lord.

He does not stumble upon her
by accident.

He finds her
by alignment.

And when he does,
the question is no longer a mystery.

It is an answer
walking beside him.

AUTHOR'S REFLECTION

A Word from Ukirah Yasmine

This book was not written to introduce a new concept, but to bring clarity to one that has long been misunderstood. The question presented in Proverbs 31:10 has been read for generations, yet often without full consideration of what it implies. The focus has remained largely on the woman — her attributes, her responsibilities, and her value — while the condition of the one who is meant to find her has received far less attention.

The intention of this work is not to shift value away from the woman, but to restore balance to the conversation. Value does not exist in isolation. It is recognized, received, and sustained within the context of alignment. When that alignment is absent, even what is clearly present may go unrecognized.

In writing this, I considered not only the text itself, but the experiences that surround it. There are individuals who have sought what they believe to be meaningful and have struggled to find it. There are also those who have lived in alignment with consistent principles and have yet to be recognized as such. Both experiences point to the same underlying issue: the difference between presence and perception.

This distinction is important because it influences how people understand themselves and their circumstances. When recognition is absent, it is easy to assume that something is lacking. However, absence of recognition does not necessarily indicate absence of value. It may instead reflect a lack of readiness or alignment in the environment in which one is operating. Understanding this can prevent unnecessary adjustment and support continued consistency in one's actions and decisions.

It is also important to acknowledge that development is a process. The qualities discussed throughout this book — discernment, trust, honor, positioning, and reverence — are not acquired instantly. They are cultivated over time through intentional effort and reflection. This means that the capacity to recognize and sustain value is not fixed. It can be developed, refined, and strengthened.

The purpose of this reflection is not to present conclusions as final, but to encourage continued examination. The question "Who can find a virtuous woman?" is not limited to a single context. It can be applied more broadly as a way of evaluating perception, alignment, and readiness in various areas of life. It invites the reader to consider not only what is being sought, but the condition from which the search is conducted.

If there is one principle that remains consistent throughout this discussion, it is that recognition is connected to development. What is seen, understood, and valued is influenced by the framework through which it is interpreted. By refining that framework, it becomes possible to identify what may have previously been overlooked.

This book does not attempt to redefine the passage in Proverbs 31, but to examine it more closely. The question it presents is not intended to create uncertainty, but to direct attention toward the qualities required to answer it. In doing so, it provides a perspective that is both practical and applicable.

As you reflect on what has been presented, the focus remains the same: not on what is absent, but on what is required to recognize what is present.

May blessings of The Most High be upon you, and may the Holy Spirit guide you to the divine mate who is equally yoked with you. Sing praises to His name Jah!

www.ingramcontent.com/pod-product-compliance
Lightning Source LLC
LaVergne TN
LVHW010940110826
845149LV00013B/2687

9783138076147